OXFORD
UNIVERSITY PRESS

Great Clarendon Street, Oxford OX2 6DP

Oxford University Press is a department of the University of Oxford.
It furthers the University's objective of excellence in research, scholarship,
and education by publishing worldwide in

Oxford New York

Auckland Cape Town Dar es Salaam Hong Kong Karachi
Kuala Lumpur Madrid Melbourne Mexico City Nairobi
New Delhi Shanghai Taipei Toronto

With offices in

Argentina Austria Brazil Chile Czech Republic France Greece
Guatemala Hungary Italy Japan Poland Portugal Singapore
South Korea Switzerland Thailand Turkey Ukraine Vietnam

Oxford is a registered trade mark of Oxford University Press
in the UK and in certain other countries

British Library Cataloguing in Publication Data

Data available

ISBN: 978-0-19-279469-7

1 3 5 7 9 10 8 6 4 2

Printed in Great Britain by CPI Group (UK) Ltd, Croydon, CR0 4YY
Paper used in the production of this book is a natural,
recyclable product made from wood grown in sustainable forests.
The manufacturing process conforms to the environmental
regulations of the country of origin.

MAGGIE PEARSON

SHORT

CHRISTMAS STORIES

OXFORD
UNIVERSITY PRESS

Contents

Room for One More

It was a winter's night, starlit and frost-bright, the coldest night of the year.

The travellers at the inn though, they were snug and warm. So many travellers! Where did they all come from? Where were they all going to sleep?

As for feeding them all! Sarah the kitchen maid was rushed off her feet.

'Clear those dishes, Sarah!'

'Can we have some more bread over here?'

'I can smell burning! Didn't I tell you to keep an eye on that stew?'

Now here were two more weary travellers at the door, a man and his young wife. The landlord shook his head. 'I've no room left,' he said. 'I'm sorry.' Shivering, he closed the door. 'The fire's going down, Sarah,' he said. 'Bring in some more wood.'

Wrapping an old blanket round her, Sarah fetched the donkey to carry the wood, came round to the front of the inn and found the man and his wife still standing there in the bitter cold.

'Do you know of anywhere else we can go?' said the man. 'We've tried every inn in town.'

6

'Come with me,' whispered Sarah. She led them round to the stable, which was tiny. On any other night there was just room inside for the donkey and Sarah to sleep. But tonight they somehow made room for the man and his wife and the donkey too.

'But where are you going to sleep, Sarah?'

'I'll find somewhere. Don't worry.'

Upstairs in the inn the travellers were sleeping four, five, six to a bed, lying top to toe like sardines. Downstairs they dozed on benches and tables or curled up on the floor by the dying fire.

Sarah worked on, washing up, damping down the fire and sweeping the crumbs from the floor as best she could without disturbing the sleeping customers. Then, tired though she was, she took the bread left over from dinner, a jug of water and a few small fried fishes and carried them round to the stable.

A voice called, 'Come in, Sarah. Don't stand out there in the cold.'

Sarah smiled and shook her head. 'There's no room for me.'

'Oh, I think we can make room for one more.'

So she crept inside and found to her surprise that there was room, for the man and his wife, her and the donkey—and one more. A new-born baby lying snug and warm among the hay in the donkey's manger. The baby opened its eyes and smiled at her. And suddenly she wasn't tired any more. She felt more like dancing. Somewhere, it seemed, there was music and voices singing,

He has come!
He is here!
Christ is born!

7

Old Ted (1)

The snow was so thick on the ground that only Ted and the vicar managed to struggle across the fields to the church that Christmas Eve for the midnight service.

They waited till close to midnight, but nobody else turned up.

'I suppose we might as well go home,' said the vicar. 'Not bother with the service.'

'What do you mean, not bother?' said Ted. 'I'm here, aren't I? If only one cow turns up at feeding time, I still feed it!'

Old Ted (2)

'What did you get for Christmas, Ted?'
     'Nothing,' said Ted.
     'Nothing at all?'
'Nothing.'
'Didn't you buy any presents?' I asked him.
He shook his head.
'Well, then—'
'I've got that many relations,' he said, 'and I never know what to get for any of them. So this year I thought I'd just send them each a cheque. I made out the cheques and on each card I wrote, Buy your own present.'
     'And you got nothing back?'
     'I might have done,' said Ted. And he grinned. 'If I hadn't forgotten to put in the cheques with the cards!'

The Voice

He was late setting out on Christmas Eve, but he'd promised them he'd be home for Christmas.

He kept thinking if he waited just a bit longer the snow would stop. But the snow didn't stop. By the time he left it was so thick on the ground that the roads were closed. He'd have to walk, but he'd save time if he took the path across the moor. So off he went, into the driving snow.

Darkness fell and he was still walking across the empty, snow-covered moor. There was no moon to see by, no star to guide him, but he'd walked this same path so many times, it took him a while to realize he was lost.

Should he turn back? Follow his own footsteps back to the place where he started? Already they were filling with snow. They'd be gone altogether long before he reached the road. There seemed to be nothing for it but to go on. So on he trudged, but with every step he was sinking knee-deep in snow. He longed to sit down and rest. But if he did, would he ever get up again?

It was then that he heard someone calling his name.

He called out, 'Who's there?' Screwing his eyes up, trying to see, but there was only the driving snow and the dark.

The voice called again.

He thought to himself, 'I know that voice,' but his mind was so fuddled by the dark and the snow and the creeping cold, he couldn't think who it might be. Still, any company was better than none. So he set off towards it.

Sometimes he thought he could see a shadowy figure moving ahead of him. Once or twice he stopped and called out, 'I'm here! Over here!' The figure stopped when he did, as if it was waiting for him to catch up, but it came no nearer.

So onward he went, following the sound of the voice that called his name, till at last he saw a light in the distance. He struggled towards it and saw his father holding a lantern to guide him the rest of the way safely home.

'Are you all right, son? I was starting to think the worst. Your mother—'

'My mother!' That was the voice he'd heard. The voice his brain had been too fuddled to recognize. What would his mother be doing out there in the cold and dark this Christmas Eve, unless—?

Suddenly he felt colder inside than when he was struggling through the snow. The words were out of his mouth before they were properly in his head. 'Is she dead?'

'Dead? No!' cried his father. 'Whatever gave you that idea? What I was going to say was, she dropped off to sleep earlier on and dreamed she saw you lost in the snow. In her dream, she said, she kept calling out to you, trying to guide you home. I kept telling her when she woke up there was no need to worry.' He smiled. 'Now you can tell her yourself.'

Flowers of the Holy Night

'Let's make the church more beautiful than ever this Christmas!' said the priest. 'I want each and every one of you children to bring something. It doesn't matter what it is. Just bring what you can.'

Soon the church was filled with evergreen branches and sprays of berries, strings of bright capsicums and baskets of oranges, paper garlands and fancy candles—even hothouse flowers.

Pepito lived with his grandmother in a flat in the centre of town. They had no garden. There wasn't an evergreen tree or bush within walking distance. And there was no money to spare for candles or garlands.

Pepito had nothing to offer to Baby Jesus.

'Only yourself.' His grandmother kissed him.

But as he made his way to the church on Christmas Eve, he saw a cluster of weeds growing in a forgotten corner.

Quickly he gathered them. Proudly he carried them into the church. Well, the priest had said, 'Bring what you can.'

'But not weeds, Pepito! Don't you know the difference between proper plants and weeds?' sneered the boys.

'What can you expect?' sighed the girls. 'He's just a stupid boy.'

But the priest said, 'I said to you, bring what you can for Baby Jesus. And Pepito brought what he could.' He put the weeds in a vase and stood it in the place of honour right next to the crib.

Next morning—Christmas morning—Pepito couldn't wait to show his grandmother his little handful of weeds in the place of honour, right next to the crib. They got to the church early but already there was such a crowd of people round the crib the two of them couldn't get near. 'Such beautiful flowers!' he heard them saying. 'Where can I buy some? I've never seen flowers quite that wonderful shade of red.'

Pepito understood at once what had happened. The priest was just being kind last evening. On Christmas morning his handful of weeds had had to make way for those beautiful flowers.

'So where are my weeds?' he asked the priest, hoping they hadn't been thrown away.

The priest smiled. 'Those are your weeds, Pepito. Come and see.'

'Those?' Pepito couldn't believe it. 'You mean those beautiful red flowers?'

The priest's smile grew wider. He nodded. 'It's a miracle. But, then, Christmas is a time for miracles, isn't it?'

The Mexicans call these flowers *flores de la noche buena*—flowers of the holy night. We call them poinsettia.

Robin Redbreast

I t was cold in the stable.

Joseph had done his best to make a fire, but there was no warmth in it. All it did was smoulder. Off he went to search for some drier wood while Mary cuddled the sleeping baby to warm him and huddled close to the dying fire. It was scarcely more now than a wisp of smoke.

She tried to lean forward, breathe some life into it, without disturbing the baby. She whispered to the ox (but softly, so as not to wake the baby), 'Help me.' A breath or two was all the fire needed.

But the ox was asleep. He didn't hear her.

She whispered to the donkey, 'Please, help me.' But the donkey, too, was sound asleep.

The fire was dying and there was no sign of Joseph.

Then a little brown bird fluttered down from the rafters. He stood for a moment with his head on one side, looking at Mary and the baby.

Then he hopped over to the fire and began to fan it with his wings.

A flame leapt up, and then another.

The little bird stopped fanning the flames just long enough to shift some twigs from the outside of the fire to the centre.

Then he hopped closer still to the flames, fanning them with his little wings as if his own life depended on it.

When Joseph came back with a fresh armful of wood, the fire was blazing merrily and the stable was snug and warm, but the poor little bird—

'Look at his breast!' whispered Mary.

The little bird's breast had been scorched red-raw by the flames.

Mary held out her finger for the bird to perch on and lifted him up.

The baby—awake now—held out his little hands towards him.

And the robin—for that's who the little brown bird was— felt the pain fading away. But his breast stayed as red as ever. And so it remains, to this day.

La Befana

La Befana lived all alone, but she wasn't lonely. She loved every one of the village children as if they were her own. She knitted and sewed and carved wooden toys for them and baked them sweets and biscuits, till their mothers cried out, 'Stop! Please stop, La Befana. You're spoiling them.'

So La Befana stopped making sweets and biscuits. She stowed away all the toys she'd made to save for birthdays and began to pour out all the love in her heart on caring for her little house. She swept and cleaned and scrubbed and polished till it was like a little palace. When three wealthy travellers arrived in the village, the villagers were in no doubt where would be the best place for them to stay the night. La Befana welcomed them in. Had they come far? she asked them.

A good few miles, they said. And they still had a long way to go, to a place called Bethlehem, to see a new-born baby boy.

'All that way, just to see a baby!' she cried.

'Ah! This is a special baby,' they told her.

'He's going to change the world!'

They showed her the gifts they were taking him, gold,

frankincense, and myrrh.

'Very nice!' she said. Privately she thought a few baby clothes might have been a better idea. And a cuddly toy or two.

Next evening—which seemed an odd time to be leaving, 'But we're following a star, you see,' they explained—the travellers set out again on their quest.

As she tidied up after them La Befana wished she'd offered them one of the toys she'd made to give to the new-born baby who was going to change the world. There was still time to go after them. Catch them up. Maybe even go with them. What an adventure that would be! But which toy should she take? This one? That one?

By the time she'd decided to take them all, make up her mind when she got there, the three travellers were long gone, but La Befana wasn't downhearted. With her basket of toys in one hand and her broom in the other (just in case the baby's mother needed a hand with the housework), she set out. She went from town to town, asking, 'Have you seen them? Three travellers, rich men, following a star?' And if the answer was No, 'Can you tell me, then, the way to Bethlehem?'

And wherever she went there were always children staring longingly at her basket of toys, till it seemed unkind not to part with just one—or two—or more. The basket grew so light, she was afraid there'd be no toys left to offer the baby, but when she looked inside—wonder of wonders!—it was still brim-full of toys!

Through the wide world they say La Befana still wanders, searching for the way to Bethlehem, still handing out toys from her basket. Somehow towards the end of December she always finds herself back in Italy, handing out sweets and toys to the children there every Christmas.

Footpsteps in the Dark

Maybe his hearing wasn't quite what it was, but the old man could have sworn he heard footsteps behind him as he came down the long, dark street. Each time he looked, there was no one there. No footprints but his own in the snow. But each time he walked on, there came that sound again, of footsteps echoing behind him. It was a relief when he came to his lodgings and let himself in just as the church clock was striking eight. He hung up his coat and went into the sitting room where, to his surprise, he found his old friend from college sitting waiting for him by the fire.

'This is a surprise!' the old man exclaimed. 'How many years has it been?'

'Too many!' his friend smiled. 'I felt I couldn't let another Christmas go by without seeing you again.'

'Well, then, Happy Christmas! Was it my landlady who let you in? How long have you been waiting? Your hands are like ice! Sit down again and I'll make up the fire. And get you a nice warm drink. A glass of mulled wine? And something to eat! You must be hungry after your journey. And here's me thinking I'd be spending Christmas alone.'

They ate, drank, talked and laughed together till well after midnight. Then his old friend lay down to sleep on a bed they'd made up on the sofa, pulling it close to the fire, for he was still icy cold.

Next morning, though the old man woke early, the sofa was empty, the pillow and covers neatly folded.

Strange, he thought, that his friend should have left without saying goodbye.

Stranger still was the untouched plate of food on the table and beside it a full glass of wine.

But they'd had a good evening together and though he spent Christmas Day alone as usual, he smiled to himself now and then, remembering. It would be good to meet up again, he thought. So a few days later he fetched out his old address book and dialled his old friend's number.

A woman answered the phone. When he asked to speak to his friend, 'I'm sorry,' she said. 'He passed away just before Christmas.'

'It must have been very sudden,' he said. An accident, perhaps, he thought, on the way home after that Christmas Eve they'd spent together.

'Oh, no,' she said, 'he'd been ill for some time. He passed away quite peacefully, in his own bed, at home, on Christmas Eve, just as the clock was striking eight. He spoke of you often,' she said. 'He was always saying the two of you should meet up again sometime.'

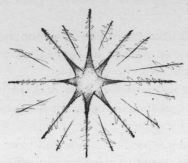

Christmas 1914

At first I thought I must be dreaming. I couldn't hear the guns, you see. I'd got so used to the sound of the guns, day and night. Now there was just these voices, singing.

It crossed my mind I might have died in the night and gone to heaven but the singing wasn't that good—not like angel voices—and besides, I thought, heaven's got to be a sight more comfortable than a muddy hole in Flanders.

Then Bert nudged me. 'Hark at that,' he said. 'Jerry's singing us Christmas carols.'

I listened for a bit, then, 'That's never the Germans,' I said. 'That's an English carol, that is. That's "Silent Night".'

'But they're not singing in English, though; are they?' he said. He was right.

Then the singing stopped and a voice from the German trenches called out. 'Hello, Tommy! Merry Christmas!'

I know Christmas is the season of goodwill and all that, but you could have knocked me down with a feather.

A few of our lads called back, 'Merry Christmas!'

After that there was silence for a bit. Then I saw our captain—a fine officer, he was, always led from the front, not like some I could name. Mad Jack we called him. Like I said,

20

I saw him take out his handkerchief and, holding it high in the air like a flag of truce, he climbed up out of the trench, slow but steady, up and over the top.

I thought, well, that's the last of Mad Jack. He was a sitting duck. I sat there listening for the sound of sniper fire. Nothing.

So after a bit I sneaked a look and blow me if Mad Jack wasn't chatting away to this German officer in the middle of no-man's-land like two pals who'd happened to meet in Trafalgar Square.

And all along the line—on their side as well as ours—there were chaps climbing out and moving forward to join them. So I went too, still half wondering if it was all a dream, till I came up against this big German fellow. He was solid enough. He smiled, so I smiled and we shook hands.

'Hello, Fritz,' I said.

'Ja! Ja! Fritz,' he said, pointing to himself.

So I told him my name and after that we got on like a house on fire, swapping cigarettes and showing each other photos of our families.

Then somebody fetched out a football. I reckon it must have been one of our chaps. I can't see anyone but an Englishman bringing a football into a battle zone on the off-chance of getting a game, can you? Anyway, we had a good old kick-about, them against us, till it was getting dark and time to go back to our trenches. Afterwards, waiting for the guns to start up again, I couldn't help thinking it was a pity we couldn't settle the war that way, then we could all go home. Except that the Jerries won. And that wouldn't do at all, would it?

The Silent Monks

There is an order of silent monks who are allowed to speak just once a year, after dinner on Christmas Day. Even then they have to take it in turns.

When it came to Brother Jerome's turn to speak, he said, 'As usual, that was a truly delicious meal. We are lucky to have such a wonderful cook.'

The next year it was Brother Michael's turn. He said, 'That was a terrible meal. As usual the potatoes were hard, the sprouts were mushy and the gravy was full of lumps. We really should change our cook.'

The year after that, Brother Timothy spoke. He said, 'I wish you two would stop bickering. You're giving me a headache.'

The Little Match-Girl

'Who'll buy my matches? Two rows for a penny. Matches! Matches! Who'll buy? Who'll buy?'

Few among the crowds hurrying by on that cold Christmas Eve even heard her. Those that did maybe glanced round once; maybe thought, 'Poor little thing, barefoot in the snow.' But they didn't need matches, not just at the moment. They'd got more important things on their minds. The turkey to collect. A bottle of wine. A couple of last-minute presents. Then home to a nice glass of hot toddy to warm them in front of a blazing log fire.

'Matches! Matches! Please buy my matches.'

She dared not go back without selling them. But the shops were closing, the streets were emptying. And she was so, so cold!

The little match-seller crouched in a doorway, pulling her skirt over her poor frozen feet, trying to warm them.

When her grandmother was alive, there would have been a fire to go home to, loving arms to hold her and her grandmother's voice singing her to sleep.

Now there was only the gang master.

How hard would he beat her if she stole just one match? Just one, she promised herself, as she struck it against the wall.

But the light of it was so beautiful—magical—and the faint touch of warmth on her hands was so sweet, she just had to light another.

And another, after that.

They flared up, bright as shooting stars in her hands.

Something made her look up, just in time to see a real shooting star travelling across the night sky.

'Someone is dying,' she whispered, for her grandmother had told her that shooting stars were the souls of the dying on their way to Paradise.

'Grandmother, I miss you so!' she whispered. 'Why did you leave me?'

Crouching there, alone in the darkness, she fancied she heard her grandmother answer, 'There, there, my love! Dry your tears. I'm here with you now.'

The last match flickered and died, but the light didn't fade. In its glow she saw her grandmother holding out her arms. 'Come to me, child. Sleep now.'

They found the little match-girl on Christmas morning, lying huddled in the doorway, with the used matches scattered around her.

'Dead of cold!'

'Poor little thing!'

'But she looks so happy—doesn't she? How strange!'

Old Ted (3)

If you go down to the barn at midnight on Christmas Eve, Ted told me, you can hear the animals talking in human voices.

'Pull the other one!' I said.

'It's true,' said Ted. 'My cousin Wilf, he heard them. Quite by accident, it was. He'd had a fair bit to drink that Christmas Eve so he climbed up into the hayloft above the barn to sleep it off before he went home.

'Next thing he knew the church clock was striking midnight. And sure enough, he could hear the cows all chatting away down below, as clear as I'm talking to you. What's more, they were talking about him.

'"Poor old Wilf!" he heard one of them say. "He's not such a bad sort."'

'That's nice to hear, thought Wilf, at the same time wondering why they thought he was "poor old Wilf". He soon got his answer.

'"Dead by morning, he'll be," says the cow.

'"Is that so?" says another.

'"Stone cold dead."

'Then they all turned their heads and looked up at the hayloft, thoughtful-like, the way cows do, and saw Wilf peering over the edge.

26

'"Oops," says the first cow. "Me and my big mouth."

'That did it! Wilf couldn't get out of there fast enough, but he was in such a tizzy, he turned the wrong way. Fell head first out of the hayloft onto the concrete floor. Stone cold dead, he was, when we found him next morning.'

'So the cows got it right,' I said. 'I wonder how they knew. Hang on a minute, though,' I said. 'If Wilf was the only one who heard them talking and he was stone cold dead when you found him, how do you know—?'

But Ted was already long gone, leaving me still wondering.

The King of Pantomime

'I'm sorry. There's nothing I can do for you.' The doctor's face was grave. 'There is no treatment—no medicine in the whole, wide world that will make you better! Because,' and here his face broke into a grin, 'because there's nothing wrong with you!'

The sad little man in front of him looked sadder still.

'Then why am I so sad?'

'You just need cheering up, that's all,' said the doctor. 'A trip to the pantomime, that's what I prescribe! Go to the pantomime at Covent Garden. Go and see Joey Grimaldi. He's the king of pantomime. The ace of clowns! I haven't laughed so much since—I don't know when!' The doctor chuckled to himself, remembering.

'Yes! Go to the pantomime!' he said. 'Grimaldi! He's the man to put you right! Now, what was your name again?'

'Grimaldi,' sighed the sad little man. 'Joey Grimaldi. Please send your bill care of the Covent Garden Theatre.'

Pantomime Crackers

What's a ghost's favourite Christmas entertainment?
A phantomime.

What's the scariest pantomime?
Ghouldilocks and the Three Bears.

What's beautiful and grey and wears glass slippers?
Cinderellephant.

On which side of the house did Jack's beanstalk grow?
The outside.

What kind of pet did Aladdin have?
A flying car-pet.

The Babes in the Wood

It's marked on the map as Wayland Wood, but Wailing Wood is its true name. The story goes that a rich man died, leaving his two orphaned children (and the money they were to inherit when they were old enough) in the care of his brother, their uncle.

The uncle wasn't a poor man himself. But he didn't like children and he did like money. So he hired two rogues to take the children deep into Wayland Wood and kill them. Rats, foxes, and maggots, he reckoned, would make short work of their bodies, leaving only their poor little bones.

His story would be that they'd wandered off into the wood to play—though he'd warned them not to—and got themselves lost. How sad!

One of the rogues was as hard-hearted as the wicked uncle, so long as the money was right, but the other one couldn't go through with it.

So they came to blows. The soft-hearted one killed the other one. Afterwards he searched in vain for the children. He had a sister living close by who'd take them in. But hand in hand and deeper into the wood they'd run in terror from the sight of the two men fighting over whether they should live or die.

They ran until they could run no longer. Tired and cold and hungry they lay down to sleep, wrapped in each other's arms.

This is the point in the pantomime where Robin Hood comes to their rescue—hurrah!

The truth is that only the woodland creatures saw them, watched them, pitied them, and the robins covered them with autumn leaves to keep them warm.

In time the rogue who hadn't had the heart to kill them was caught for another crime and, to save himself from the hangman's rope, confessed his part in the disappearance of the rich man's two orphaned children.

The wicked uncle was thrown in jail, in the deepest, darkest, dampest, smelliest dungeon that could be found. But that was no comfort to those two poor little children he'd wronged.

Search parties were sent out to scour the wood and were led, so they said, to the place where they lay by the sound of crying. Which was strange because, in spite of the coverlet of autumn leaves, by that time the two little babes in the wood were stone cold dead.

Still, they say, if you walk through Wayland Wood on a winter's day when the leaves have fallen, you can still hear the sound of those two poor little children crying carried on the winter wind.

The Coming of Winter

Brightest and best of all the gods was Baldur the beautiful, the beloved. Surely nothing on earth would wish to ever harm him. Still Frigg worried about him, the way all mothers do.

Through the wide world she went, begging each thing, living and non-living, animals, plants, rocks, the four winds, the waves of the sea and the shooting stars in the sky, 'Promise me you will never hurt my son.'

Patiently, from the shadows, Loki watched her—Loki the trickster, the trouble-maker—and saw that there was one thing she'd missed. The mistletoe—so small, so weak!—clinging to the oak trees' highest branches.

In the gods' hall of Asgard, the young gods set Baldur up as a target. Baldur the beautiful, the beloved—the invincible! They threw spears at him, fired arrows, hurled rocks and marvelled to see how they all fell short. They attacked him with swords and axes. The blades simply glanced aside.

Blind Hodur stood apart, listening, wishing he could join in the fun.

'You can,' whispered Loki. 'I'll help you.' He pressed a dart made from mistletoe into Hodur's hand. 'Let me guide you. All you have to do is draw your arm back and throw—now!'

The mistletoe dart flew straight to Baldur's heart.

As the gods saw him fall there was a deathly silence in the hall of Asgard.

'Did I hit him?' asked Hodur.

'You hit him,' murmured Loki. 'Well done, Hodur. You hit him and you killed him. Baldur is dead.'

Weeping, Frigg went to Hel, goddess of the underworld. 'Give me back my son!' she begged. 'All the world mourns for Baldur. Please send him back.'

Her tears softened even proud Hel's heart. 'Does all the world truly mourn for Baldur?' she said. 'If that is so, then I will send him back to you.'

And all the world did mourn for Baldur. The trees shed their leaves and the rivers froze over and the gods tore their hair and wept. All except Loki.

He said, 'Frigg thought she could make Baldur proof against death. I proved her wrong. Why should I weep at that?'

Then the gods took Loki and bound him with chains to a rock deep under the earth where a foul serpent dripped acid poison on him night and day.

Drip—drip—drip.

Loki screamed as the acid burned him.

'Mourn for Baldur,' they told him, 'and we'll set you free.'

'Never!' roared Loki.

So every winter the world mourns for Baldur. The trees shed their leaves, the earth covers itself in a shroud of snow and the rivers freeze over. The wind howls and the sky weeps and the mistletoe is strung with Frigg's tears.

Dathera Dad

A farmer's wife was making a Christmas pudding. She mixed flour and suet and sugar and eggs. Stirred in raisins and almonds, a dollop of treacle and a generous helping of brandy. She called in the children so they could take it in turns to stir the pudding while they made a Christmas wish. Lastly she added a silver sixpence and a lucky charm for each one of the family.

Then she wrapped the pudding in a muslin cloth, tied it up tight and dropped it into the copper to boil.

As the pudding bobbed about in the boiling water it made a noise as if it was singing. 'Dathera Dad,' it sang. 'Dathera Dad.'

When the pudding was done, the farmer's wife took it out of the water and hung it up by the window to cool.

Who should happen by then but a hungry tinker.

He saw the pudding hanging there, like a big juicy fruit, just ripe for picking. Next thing, he was off down the road, with the pudding bobbing by his side. And the pudding began to sing again, 'Dathera Dad. Dathera Dad!'

The tinker stopped.

'Dathera Dad!' sang the pudding. 'Take me home to my Dathera Dad!'

The tinker dropped it. The bag split open. The pudding was scattered all over the road.

There stood a teeny tiny man.

He scowled up at the startled tinker and stamped his foot.

'I said, take me home to my Dathera Dad!' he yelled.

Then he ran off down the road.

And was never seen or heard of again.

The Christmas Tree

'Be happy, little fir tree,' whispered the sun. 'Look at the beautiful world around you. The birds, the butterflies, the flowers, the trees.'

There must be more to life than this, thought the little fir tree.

'What more could you want?' sighed the rain. 'You're young and strong and still growing and free to enjoy each day as it comes.'

The little fir tree still wanted more. In summer the loggers came to cut down the tallest, straightest trees to be turned into masts for ships which, so the swallows told him, would sail across the sea to the ends of the earth and beyond. The little fir tree stretched himself as tall as he could. 'Take me!' he begged. 'Take me!' Of course they never did. He was much too small.

Then the sparrows whispered to him of a much more glorious destiny—so glorious, it was hard to believe. 'But we've seen it!' they twittered. 'Last Christmas. A tree no bigger than you, carried inside a human house to be decked in gold and silver, with candles burning on every branch.'

The little fir tree could hardly believe his luck when Christmas came round again and he heard a little girl say,

36

'Yes! That one!'

The axe severed his trunk with a single blow that hurt so much that he fainted, thinking not of the glory to come, only the sadness of leaving the forest behind.

When he came to himself again, he was standing in a bucket of sand and the horizon had shrunk to four solid walls. But it was true, what the sparrows had told him, about being decked out in gold and silver with candles burning on every branch. There were toys, too, and baskets of sweets. 'I look so beautiful!' the little fir tree told himself, preening himself in the mirror over the fireplace.

That evening, Christmas evening, all around him there was dancing and merriment and games. One by one the children snatched the toys and sweets from his branches until, snatching a look at himself in the mirror again, the little fir tree did think he looked a bit the worse for wear. His needles on one side were quite singed from standing so close to the fire. The sand in the bucket had dried out and he was so, so thirsty.

Still the little fir tree held his head up proudly. This was better than life in the forest! Wasn't it? A small voice inside him whispered, 'No!'

'Well, that's it!' said the servants as they carried the Christmas tree out to the rubbish heap next morning. 'That's Christmas over for another year.'

Was that it? he thought. Was that all? Surely there must be something more.

'Wait a minute!' cried the cook.

'I knew it!' thought the fir tree. 'My story's not ended yet.'

But all stories must end. The little fir tree's ended in one last blaze of glory on the kitchen fire.

The Ogre Who Stole the Sun

There was an ogre who stole the sun. He didn't want it. He didn't need it. He just liked giving people a hard time.

He shut the sun away in a box, while the people crept about in darkness. The crops withered in the fields. There was not enough light from the moon and the stars to hunt by. Soon they were pretty near starving.

So they went to Raven, the wise, the shape-shifter. 'Help us!' they begged him.

Next morning—if it was morning; how could anyone tell? Not even the ogre, who only took the sun out now and then to gloat over his ill-gotten gains.

Let's call it morning.

What did the ogre find on his doorstep but a baby!

Like a lot of big, clumsy men, he was a bit of a softie where babies were concerned.

'Poor little thing!' he said. 'Left all alone in the cold.'

So he took it inside. He fed it. He changed it.

The baby started to cry, 'Wah! Wah! Wah!'

The ogre picked the baby up. It cried louder.

He rocked it. He sang to it. He pulled funny faces and jiggled it up and down on his knee.

'Wah! Wah! Wah!' yelled the baby.

Just now and then it paused in its crying to watch the flames of the fire flickering over the walls of the ogre's cave.

Then, 'Wah! Wah! Wah!' It was off again.

Of course! thought the ogre. Babies always love bright, shiny things. What had he got that was bright and shiny?

Of course! The very thing!

He opened up the lid of the box where he'd hidden the sun.

The baby stopped crying at once. It held out its dear little arms.

'Goo–goo-goo!' it chuckled.

'Here you are!' smiled the ogre.

'Goo-goo-goo!' chuckled Raven, seizing the sun from the ogre's outstretched hands. Changing back into his true shape he soared up through the smoke hole to return the sun to its proper place in the sky.

The ogre roared.

The people cheered.

Raven circled once—twice—three times round in triumph. Then on his raven's wings he flew away in search of fresh adventures.

The Legend of the Christmas Rose

She was tired out after helping her father all day, fetching the stray sheep down from the hills above Bethlehem.

It was going to be a cold night, he said. If the sheep weren't brought in under cover, they'd surely die.

Too tired even to eat, she fell asleep. And was woken the next minute, it seemed, by voices singing in the sky above.

By the time she'd rubbed the sleep from her eyes, the voices had gone, leaving her thinking it had maybe been just a dream. But something was up. It was the middle of the night still, but everyone was moving about.

'Come on, then, if you're coming,' said her father.

'Come where?' she yawned.

'Down to the town.'

'Down to the town? Why? Is everyone going? What about the sheep?'

'They'll be fine with the dogs to guard them.'

Still yawning, still rubbing the sleep from her eyes, she followed the shepherds down to the town.

Through the dark, sleeping streets they went, whispering softly among themselves, till they came to a stable behind an inn. Through the doorway she saw a woman holding a newborn baby in her arms.

One by one the shepherds crept inside the stable.

She saw now that each of them was carrying a present for the baby. A fleece, a small wooden carving, or a cheese made from sheep's milk.

She'd brought nothing. She didn't know you had to bring a present. She knelt on the ice-hard ground and cried and cried till she felt her father's hand on her shoulder. 'Why are you crying?' he asked her.

'Because I've got nothing to bring the baby.'

'Why don't you bring him these?'

She looked down and saw that wherever her tears had fallen, a flower was growing, creamy-white.

Quickly she gathered them and carried them into the stable.

Shyly she offered them to the lady, who took them with a smile and showed them to the baby, who laughed and held out his little hands to touch them.

And that's how the first Christmas roses came into the world.

The Ring

He'd meant to get his wife something for Christmas. Something special, he told himself, not just chocolates or perfume. Something that showed he'd really given it some thought.

But while he was thinking about it, Christmas crept up on him. Now it was Christmas Eve, he'd still got nothing and all the shops were shut.

But, as luck would have it, his journey home took him past the old churchyard by the sea. The church had long ago been washed away by the waves and the graves were following it one by one. There'd been a storm the night before that had washed more of the soil away. And there, sticking out of the ground—what luck!—was a skeletal hand with a rather handsome ring on its finger.

One quick glance round, and the ring was in his pocket and he was hurrying home. His wife was delighted. 'It's beautiful! I'm never going to take it off.' When they went to bed she was still wearing it.

In the middle of the night she woke, to hear a voice calling from under the window, 'Give it back! Give me back what you stole from me.'

She nudged her husband. 'There's someone out in the

garden.'

'Take no notice,' he mumbled. 'Go back to sleep.'

She tried to sleep, but then she heard the same voice out on the landing, 'Give it back! Give me back what you stole from me.'

She nudged her husband again. 'There's someone in the house.'

'Rubbish,' he said, turning over. 'Go back to sleep.'

She tried, but next time she heard it the voice was louder. 'Give it back! Give me back what you stole from me. Give it back! I'm at the foot of your bed.'

She shook her husband awake this time. 'There's someone in the room.'

'Don't talk nonsense!' He tried to pull the covers over himself, but something snatched them away. He could feel it climbing over him and he could hear the voice now, 'Give it back! Give it back! Give me back the thing that you stole from me!'

His wife cried out, 'Help! It's got me!' Bony fingers were clutching her, twining themselves in her hair.

'I will have it back!' cried the voice. 'If I have to, I'll take you with me!'

The man shouted out. 'It's the ring it wants. Get rid of the ring!'

The wife plucked the ring off her finger and flung it as far away from her as she could.

The fingers let go of her hair. There was a scuttling on the far side of the room. Then from the outside the window they heard a sound like the rattling of dry bones.

After that, silence.

'My goodness! What was *that*?' said the wife.

'I'll tell you in the morning,' he said. 'Go back to sleep.'

The Tomte's Porridge

'I can't explain it,' said the farmer. 'I go out to fetch in the cows for milking and find them all lined up ready in the barn. The horse never seems to need grooming these days and the yard's always swept and tidy. I notice a fence wants mending. By the time I've fetched my tools, it's been done.'

'It's the same inside the house,' said his wife. 'I hardly need to lift a duster. Oh, and it's lovely to come downstairs on a frosty morning and find the fire blazing away.'

'And there's just the two of you on the farm?' said their friend.

'Just the two of us.'

'You never get the impression that you might be three? I'm talking about no more than a movement glimpsed out of the corner of your eye, maybe?'

'Well, now you come to mention it—' said the farmer.

'I thought it was just the cat,' said his wife. 'Except he seemed to be wearing a hat.'

'A red hat?'

'Yes! How did you know?'

'That clinches it. You've got a tomte living with you.'

'A tomte! Is that good or bad?'

'It's good—so long as you treat him right.'

'How do we do that?'

'That's easy. A tomte doesn't ask for much. Just a dish of porridge on Christmas Eve with a pat of butter on top. Whatever you do, don't forget the butter.'

Come Christmas Eve, the farmer's wife made the porridge and left it to cool for a bit so it didn't melt the butter. She was just going to spoon it into a bowl for the tomte when the farmer said, 'What about the cat? If we leave the butter on top of the porridge, the cat might eat it.'

'I'll put the butter under the porridge,' said his wife. So that's what she did.

Of course the tomte didn't know that. There was his porridge. Where was the butter? 'Where's my butter!' he yelled.

He went ballistic. He emptied the hay store all over the yard, tied knots in the horse's mane and tail, let out the sheep and chased them all over the countryside. After all that exercise he was hungrier than ever, so he ate the porridge anyway. And found the pat of butter safe at the bottom.

Then he felt really bad.

He spent the rest of the night rounding up the sheep, clearing up the hay from the yard and untying the knots in the horse's mane and tail. Last thing of all he remembered to light the kitchen fire so it was blazing merrily when the farmer and his wife came downstairs on Christmas morning.

Christmas 1752

A right pickle we were in that year. If I tell you none of us knew what day it was, that's no more than the honest truth.

There was some bigwig up in London, you see, who'd got it into his noddle that the calendar was all wrong and it was up to the government to set it right. So they passed a law that said September 2nd would be followed that year by September 14th.

Well! You can imagine the to-do. Paying taxes was bad enough. Now the government had stolen eleven days of our lives!

There were people rioting in the streets.

'Give us back our eleven days!' they cried.

Then somebody pointed out it was a lot more serious than that. How would we know when to celebrate Christmas? What would happen if we got it wrong? Plague, maybe, and famine, said the doom-and-gloom merchants. Maybe even the end of the world!

I don't know who it was who first thought of the Glastonbury thorn. There's this old story, you see, of how, when Jesus was a nipper, his Uncle Joseph brought him to England. They stopped for a rest at Wearyall Hill by

Glastonbury. For some reason, Joseph stuck his walking stick in the ground and before they were on their way again that stick had taken root and blossomed. So they left it there. I suppose it wasn't much use as a walking stick any more. Every Christmas Day since then, so they say—not a day sooner, nor later—that bush has burst into flower. So off we all went to Glastonbury. Come the new Christmas Eve there were hundreds of us from far and wide, watching and waiting to see if that bush would bloom next morning.

Of course it didn't. The church bells rang out, but we knew it wasn't really Christmas. So we settled down to wait. Not all of us stayed, of course. It's no fun camping out in the middle of winter. But a tidy few of us had come prepared. Some just sat watching that bush, day after day. I told them a watched pot never boils, but I might as well have saved my breath.

Eleven days they sat there waiting, while the rest of us were having a high old time, singing and drinking and dancing, like it was Christmas already, which it wasn't of course.

Come Christmas morning—I mean the *real* Christmas morning, eleven days later—we woke up to find that bush had burst into blossom overnight while no one was watching it. (I felt like telling the bush-watchers, Told you so!)

But the doom-and-gloom merchants got it all wrong. The sky didn't fall in. There was no plague, no famine. So in the end those bigwigs in London got their way. But I reckon Jesus doesn't mind very much when we celebrate his birthday. Just so long as we do celebrate it, that's the main thing.

The Wolf

The way he told it, I knew the stranger we met in the pub had to be the hero of the story he told us that Christmas Eve. It was a tale, he said, of the land of his birth, a country of wide grasslands where a man might ride all day and never see another human soul. Of savage mountains and dark pine forests out of which, one winter, a rogue wolf came that didn't run with a pack but crept alone into villages by night to steal chickens and geese. And how long would it be before a child was taken?

At last some six or eight stout-hearted fellows got together and went up to the castle, offering to hunt down the beast if the young lord would lead them. Though the preparations for Christmas were well under way and his mother begged him not to go, 'It is my duty to go!' the young lord cried. 'Fetch me my rifle and my hunting dogs!'

So off they went. For mile after weary mile they tracked the creature through the snow. By day and by night, thanks to a full moon shining, through the forest and up into the mountains, till at last they had the beast cornered in a narrow ravine. Such a fight there was then! The hunting dogs were tossed aside, their throats ripped out or their backs broken. One—two—three of the villagers were savagely mauled while the young lord sought in vain for a clear shot for his rifle. Then, as the monster leapt for his throat, he brought it down with a single bullet.

The carcass was too big to carry back, so to prove that the wolf was dead the young lord cut off one of its forepaws, wrapped it in a cloth and put it in his hunting bag. It was a long, slow journey down the mountain, carrying the injured men, but as the bells were ringing out on Christmas morning they reached the village, where they were received with great rejoicing. At the height of which the young lord opened his bag and unwrapped the wolf's paw, holding it aloft for all to see. At which the cheers died away—and he saw that what he held up was not a wolf's paw, but a severed human hand!

'Are you telling us he'd killed a werewolf?' Jack grinned, disbelieving.

'But I thought a werewolf could only be killed with a silver bullet,' I said.

'That's true,' the stranger told us, smiling.

'So was it really dead?' I asked him.

'Who knows? All I can tell you for sure is that the creature was never seen in those parts again.'

I wanted to ask him then about other stuff I'd read. That a werewolf's power is strongest at Christmas time and when there's a full moon shining. Didn't that make it more likely that the creature wasn't dead after all?

But already he was getting up to go. It was then, as he slipped on his coat, that I noticed his left hand was missing. 'A hunting accident,' he shrugged. 'Many years ago, back in my homeland. It's a fine night,' he said. 'And a full moon. Would either of you care to walk with me part of the way?'

Old Ted (4)

'I've been thinking,' said Ted, 'about Father Christmas.'

'What about him?' I said.

'I reckon he could be a vampire,' said Ted.

'A vampire?' I said. 'Father Christmas?'

'Just think about it,' he said. 'How old is Father Christmas?'

'Centuries!' I said. 'He's immortal.'

'Put it another way,' said Ted. 'Could it be, he's one of the Undead? He never goes out in sunlight, does he? He only comes out at night. Just like a vampire. How does he get into a house?'

'Down the chimney, of course.'

'And how does a big feller like him manage that without turning himself into something very small? A bat, maybe? That's the vampire's favourite!'

'You said a big feller,' I said. 'I thought vampires were supposed to be skinny.'

'You don't know what's under that red coat,' said Ted. 'Could be most of it's just padding. And why do you think the coat's always red?'

'I know you're going to tell me.'

'That's to hide the fresh blood. What's that big bushy beard for if it's not to hide his pointy vampire teeth?'

'So what about the presents?' I said. 'Vampires don't go round handing out presents.'

'Ah!' said Ted. 'There you've got me. I'm still working that bit out. Maybe he's a reformed vampire.'

Old Ted (5)

'You're looking very down in the mouth, Ted.'

'It's my nephew,' he said. 'He's in trouble again.'

That was nothing new. Ted's nephew's more often in trouble than out of it.

'What's he been up to this time?'

'He says he was just trying to get his Christmas shopping done early. Get in there ahead of the crowds.'

'That's not a crime, is it?'

Ted shook his head. 'It is,' he said, 'if the police catch you inside the shop before it's open.'

The Big White Cat

Their mother, so it was said, had been a troll who ate naughty children and though the Yule Boys never ate anybody, they still terrorized the countryside for miles around, especially at Christmas.

One poor man decided he'd had enough. He was loading up the cart to take his family into town for the holidays, when a travelling man came down the road with a great white bear plodding behind him.

'Don't mind him,' said the travelling man. 'He's just a great big pussycat at heart. I see you're going away for Christmas,' he said. 'Would you like us to keep an eye on the place while you're away?'

That was an offer the farmer couldn't refuse! Off he went with his wife and family, while the travelling man made himself at home, with supper spread out on the table and the bear spread out in front of the fire, like a lumpy bearskin rug.

It wasn't long before the Yule Boys were up to their tricks. First came a scratching at the window. Then came a hammering on the door, followed by a patter of footsteps on the roof. When smoke began billowing down the chimney the travelling man strode to the door and flung it open. 'Come on in, lads,' he roared. 'We're ready for you!'

Maybe the Yule Boys should have stopped to wonder what exactly he meant by that, but their minds were too set on wrecking the place, in between stuffing as much food as they could into their mouths without choking and making enough noise to wake the dead or maybe even a sleeping bear.

The bear stirred. He growled.

'Don't mind him,' said the man. 'He's just a great, big pussycat at heart.'

'A pussycat?' cried the Yule Boys. 'We love pussycats!'

But then the bear stood up. And he was huge!

He yawned and his throat was like an endless, bright-red tunnel, wide enough to swallow any one of the Yule Boys whole. If not, those teeth were big and sharp enough to snap them into bite-size pieces.

He stretched, sending them flying and tumbling every which way, bumping their heads and snapping their bones.

Those Yule Boys couldn't get out of there fast enough, up the chimney, through the windows, fighting one another to be first through the door.

Next year as the farmer was out tending his sheep, he heard a voice calling to him, 'Is that travelling man and big white cat still living with you?'

'No,' said the farmer, 'but we've invited them both back for Christmas. I did hear she's had kittens since last year and one of them's promised to each of my neighbours.'

The Yule Boys were soon reformed characters after that. These days they're welcome visitors. When they come down from the hills at Christmas, they come carrying presents to tuck into the shoes Icelandic children leave on the windowsill.

Always Look on the Bright Side

There was a man who had two sons and they couldn't have been more different from one another.

One always looked on the bright side. He was what's called an optimist.

The other was just the opposite. He was a pessimist.

After several miserable Christmases, with the pessimist son always moaning about this or that or the other thing, the father splashed out and bought this boy everything he could possibly want.

And—maybe as a test; maybe for a joke—the father got a bucket of horse dung and left it in the other boy's room.

Come Christmas morning, the pessimist son was in floods of tears, all his dream-toys scattered round him. 'How am I going to cope with all this stuff?' he cried. 'I'll never have time to play with it all. How am I going to follow all the instructions? And my friends are going to be so jealous! They're going to really, really hate me, when they see all this stuff I've got.'

The father went into the room next door and found the optimist son dancing round the bucket of horse dung. He was thrilled to bits. 'Where there's dung,' he cried, 'there's got to be a pony. Right, Dad?'

I hope there was.

First Snow

In the days when men and women first came into the world, life was good. The sun shone, the rain fell softly and mostly at night. The maize grew tall, squash swelled, berries hung thick and ripe ready for picking and the fish in the rivers and lakes more or less jumped out of the water into your hand.

Then Sky Father said, 'These people have it too easy!' He sent the first snow to cover the land.

The people huddled together in the cold. 'Help us, Earth Mother!' they cried. 'The world is dying.'

Earth Mother smiled. 'The world is not dying,' she said. 'The world is sleeping, renewing itself. Under that blanket of snow, fresh seeds are sprouting. Next year the corn will grow as tall as ever. The squash and berries will come again. Did you think the rivers would run for ever? The rivers would run dry if the snow didn't fall on the mountains. In spring the snow will melt and refresh the rivers.'

'But how shall we live until spring comes?'

'Do you see the animal tracks in the snow? See how easy it is to follow them—to hunt them down. I will teach you to make fire, so you can cook the animals you kill. I will teach you to skin them to make clothes for yourselves against the cold. And when spring comes—as it will come—the world will look even more beautiful than it did before.'

Sky Father said, 'You spoil them, Earth Mother.'

'Earth Mother said, 'Watch them. You should be proud of them. They're our children. See how quickly they learn.'

The Snow Maiden

ather Frost loves children. When winter comes the grown-ups huddle inside their winter coats and fur-lined boots and hurry home to stoke up the stove. But for children winter is beautiful. Winter is magical. Winter is a time to play in the snow. To throw snowballs and build snowmen. To skate on frozen ponds and rivers and toboggan down hillsides with Father Frost nipping their noses and ears (but only in a playful way).

Overnight he draws frost pictures on the window panes for the children to wonder at when they wake before their mothers rub the pictures away.

Yes, Father Frost loves children. He longed for a child of his own. So he fashioned a child out of snow. A snow maiden, slender as a birch tree and beautiful as the world in winter. He set a crown of snowflakes in her hair and breathed life into her with his icy breath.

All winter he watched as she played in the deep woods day after day. The snow maiden was never bored. Everything in this brave new world she found herself in was wonderful and strange. The shape of a pinecone, the stars in the sky, the song of a robin.

The snow maiden was never lonely. She had the woodland

creatures for her friends. The snow maiden was never sad until the day a sound came stealing through the forest, like nothing she'd ever heard before.

A cold tear ran down her cheek, but still she stood listening, letting the music wrap itself around her drawing her towards it, to the very edge of the forest. And there she saw a creature like herself—but so unlike! His cheeks were pink and his eyes were blue and his hair as dark as a blackbird's wing.

The shepherd boy stopped playing his flute as soon as he saw her, a girl as slender as a birch tree, beautiful as the world in winter and white as snow.

'Who are you?' he called out. 'Are you a ghost?'

'Play again!' whispered the snow maiden. 'Please play again.'

'Come closer, then, where I can see you. Come out into the sunlight.'

So the snow maiden stepped out into the sunlight, tears of happiness and sadness running down her cheeks.

The shepherd boy picked up his pipe to play again, but already the snow maiden was melting before his eyes.

In vain Father Frost tried to breathe life into his little daughter again, but the winter was over. His powers were too weak.

Still, every winter Father Frost grows strong. Then the snow maiden lives again and comes to help him deliver Christmas and New Year presents to Russian girls and boys.

After the Dance

I met her at the Christmas dance.

We used to have proper dances in those days, none of your discos but real, live music and dances where you had to know the steps. The boys all wore their Sunday suits and the girls had these tight-waisted, full-skirted dresses.

She was the prettiest girl there.

I couldn't believe my luck when I plucked up the courage to ask her to dance and she let me lead her onto the dance floor.

She was so light on her feet it was like dancing with my own shadow. I picked up a strand of tinsel that had fallen from the Christmas tree and gave it to her to twine in her long, blonde hair.

'You're my princess,' I whispered.

She said, 'I knew tonight would be special. I wasn't going to let anything keep me away.'

All evening we danced together and when the last waltz was over, I asked if I could see her home.

'Oh, I've got my bike,' she said.

'So have I,' I said. 'I'll ride along with you.'

But when we got to the cycle rack, her bike wasn't there.

'I'm sure I left it just here,' she said. 'At least, I think I did.'

'Someone's taken it by mistake,' I said, not wanting to spoil the evening by suggesting it might have been stolen. 'Never mind. Hop on and I'll give you a lift.'

So off we went, the two of us on my bike, her perched on the carrier behind me with her arms around my waist and her head resting on my shoulder. The moon was up and the stars were out, but when we got to the towpath down by the river—

'It's dark along here,' she said. 'So dark!'

'Not to worry,' I said. 'I can see the way. But hang on tight, the ice here is slippery.'

'I know,' she said. 'I know.'

Then I saw lights up ahead, an ambulance and a police car. There were men standing waist-deep in the river, though the water must have been near freezing.

They were lifting something out of the water.

A girl's bike.

Then they were lifting something else. Something that must have been trapped underneath it. Something that made my heart stand still.

'Don't look,' I said. But even before I looked behind me, I knew she was gone. The feel of her arms around my waist, the weight of her head resting on my shoulder, even the warm body-scent of her were gone—all gone.

'She must have been on her way to the dance,' they said.

'Such a pity she never made it.'

They lifted her out of the water, laid her body on a stretcher and covered her face with a blanket, but not before I had seen the string of tinsel I'd given her still twined in her long, blonde hair.

Stargazy Pie

I n those days if you lived by the sea, you lived off the sea. When the winter storms came and it was too rough for the fishing boats to put out from Mousehole harbour, we had to make do with what we could grow. Potatoes and turnips mostly. And cabbage.

The storms came early that year and stayed on. Midwinter's Day came and went and still the boats were stuck in harbour. They said that particular storm might blow itself out come Christmas Day, but what good was that? No fisherman would put to sea on Christmas Day, any more than he would on a Sunday. We were all sick to death of cabbage and turnips by then, but it looked like that's what our Christmas dinner would be.

Then, two days before Christmas, first thing in the morning, the word ran round the village, Tom Bawcock's boat was gone. And Tom with it!

It was a brave thing for him to do, but a foolish one. It was still blowing a gale out there. Some of those waves were as high as a house. We never expected to see Tom Bawcock again.

Still, while there's life there's hope, so they say. So the whole village hoped and prayed that he'd come back safe to harbour. Relays of men were sent up to watch for him from the top of the cliff and came back down wet through and pale as death from the cold, like dead men, drowned.

Then, as daylight was fading, a shout came from the clifftop. 'It's him!'

Some people shouted back up, disbelieving, 'It never is!'

The man who'd been stationed up on the cliff came running down to tell us. 'It is! That's Tom Bawcock's boat. I'd know it anywhere.'

He was right.

There was Tom Bawcock, sailing his boat back into the safety of Mousehole harbour, triumphant. And with such a catch of fish on board and their little heads sticking out through the net, as if to say, 'Here we are! Merry Christmas!'

There was enough to feed the whole village, though mind you, it was a pretty mixed bag. Tom made sure it was all shared out fairly. My mam came home with seven kinds of fish. She laid them out on the kitchen table. There were sand eels, mackerel, dogfish, pilchards, herring, ling and one other that none of us could put a name to. It tasted all right, though. My mam baked them all in a pie with the pilchards' heads sticking out, as if they were gazing up at the stars.

That stargazy pie was so good, we've been cooking it ever since down Mousehole way.

And we've renamed the day in Tom's honour. December the twenty-third. Tom Bawcock's Day, we call it.

Baker's Dozen

'A dozen biscuits, if you please.'
The baker counted them, popped them in a bag and held his hand out for the money.
'But that's only twelve,' the old woman said. 'The baker up the road always puts in one extra.'

'More fool him,' said the baker, 'if he wants to go broke giving away free biscuits. But I've got a family to keep. A dozen means twelve and that's what I've given you.'

Well, the old woman paid up. She snatched the bag from him and left the shop mumbling crossly to herself.

From that day on things went badly for the baker. The bread wouldn't rise and the biscuits were burnt more often than not. His cakes, which used to be light as a feather, were now as heavy as lead. As for his pastry! He lost count of the number of customers who came back to complain they'd cracked their teeth on it.

It's that old woman! he thought. She's cursed me!

Now Christmas was coming. He should have had orders from all over town for puddings and pies and cakes and biscuits. But this year he hadn't a single order. Still, it was Christmas. So he baked a batch of St Nicholas biscuits to put in the window. He mixed the dough as carefully as he knew how. Added cinnamon, ginger, cloves, cardamom and nutmeg. That night he prayed to St Nicholas. 'St Nicholas, help me! Please let these biscuits turn out right.'

Next morning he rolled out the biscuits, stamped each one with a picture of St Nicholas and stood counting the minutes while they cooked.

And they were perfect!

The baker fell on his knees. 'Thank you, St Nicholas!' Then the shop bell rang. He had a customer. He looked up.

There was St Nicholas himself! Standing there in his bishop's robes! 'I gather you've been having a bit of trouble,' he said.

So the baker explained about the old woman—the old witch!—and how she'd cursed him for not giving her one extra biscuit on top of the dozen she'd paid for.

'Would one extra biscuit really ruin you?' said St Nicholas. 'Think about it.'

The baker thought about it. He hung his head. 'I suppose not,' he said. The shop bell rang again. St Nicholas had gone. There was the old woman standing there.

'I'll have a dozen biscuits, if you please,' she said.

The baker counted out a dozen St Nicholas biscuits. Then he popped in one more. The old woman took them with a smile. And from that day on his bread dough rose as it should, his cakes were feather-light and his melt-in-the-mouth pastry was famous for miles around. And whenever anyone asked him for a dozen of anything, he always popped in one extra. Just for luck.

The Brave Little Camel

'Mama! Mama!' The camel caravan had been travelling all day and the littlest camel's legs were so short, he'd had to run twice as hard as the rest just to keep up. 'Mama! Mama! Are we nearly there?'

His mother said, 'We're nearly there. I can see the oasis now, in the distance.' When they reached it, the littlest camel sank down exhausted and fell asleep, while the drivers unloaded the rest of the camel train and the three travellers who were paying for it all spent the evening looking up at the stars, making very difficult, mathematical calculations before deciding which way the caravan was to head the next day.

Early next morning, before the sun was up, while the stars were still shining, the caravan was on its way again, with the littlest camel running as fast as he could to keep up.

So on and on they went, day after day, till it seemed as if he'd always been running and always would until the day he could run no more. The littlest camel never complained. He only asked now and then, 'Mama! Are we nearly there?'

Until one day, it was getting near evening and still the camel train showed no sign of stopping to rest for the night and the littlest camel was thinking he couldn't go another step when they came to an inn on the outskirts of a village.

He heard someone say, 'This is it! This is the place.'

Then another voice. Someone was bending over him. 'You've done well, little camel! Now you shall have your reward.'

The littlest camel looked up. He saw a nice warm stable, with soft straw to sleep on and a manger full of hay. Oh, yes! he thought. That would be nice. That would be very nice! To sleep in a proper stable with all the hay he could eat. But instead they were loading him up with boxes! Just three of them, but all the same—what sort of reward was this?

'Go on, little camel.' His mother nudged him. 'I wish I was going with you.'

He let himself be led forward and was astonished to see the three men who'd brought the caravan all this way kneeling before a new-born baby lying in the manger. The littlest camel knelt too, so they could take the three packages from his back to offer to the baby.

The baby's mother held him up so he could stroke the littlest camel's nose and he was filled with such happiness that even to this day the littlest camel still brings presents to Syrian children, in memory of that night when he delivered the first Christmas presents.

Animal Crackers

How do cats greet each other at Christmas?
A furry merry Christmas and a happy mew year.

What do angry mice send each other at Christmas?
Cross mouse cards.

What do monkeys sing at Christmas?
Jungle bells, jungle bells!

What do reindeer hang on their Christmas trees?
'Horn'-aments.

Seeing's Believing

'I don't believe in Father Christmas,' she said. 'I don't believe in the Tooth Fairy, the Easter Bunny, or little green men from Mars.'

'What about ghosts?' he said. 'Do you believe in ghosts?'

'Of course not,' she said. 'Do you?'

'Oh, yes,' he said. And vanished, right in front of her eyes.

The Fir Tree

The little fir tree stood proud and tall, the only evergreen for miles around. Well, to be truthful, not so very tall, in fact he was rather on the short side compared to the trees around him. But he had every right to be proud of his green needles in winter when all the trees around had lost their leaves.

But then as the seasons turned again and all the trees were dressed first in their new spring leaves, then in their summer dress and finally in their autumn colours, the little fir tree wished he could change as they did, especially in autumn. How beautiful they all were in their different shades of gold.

'If only I could have leaves of gold!' he wished.

Always be careful what you wish for; you never know who might be listening. Night came. The little fir tree slept. And when he woke up next morning, his needles had turned to purest gold. He twisted and turned, admiring himself in the sunlight.

Then a man came along, took one look at the little fir tree in all its finery and set about stripping off the golden pine needles, popping them into the bag he carried, every single one.

Now the poor little tree had no leaves at all.

Oh, why didn't I wish for leaves of glass! he wondered. I would still look beautiful in the sunlight and no one would want to steal them from me.

Be careful what you wish for!

Night came. The little fir tree slept again. And when he woke up next morning he found himself covered in leaves of glass that glistened and sparkled in the sunlight. But then storm clouds began to gather. The sun disappeared. The wind blew and the rain poured down. When the storm was over, the leaves of glass were shattered all over the ground.

'Why didn't I just wish to be like the other trees around me?' the little tree cried.

Night came. The little fir dreamt for a third time. When he woke, he was covered with broad green leaves, like the rest of the trees of the forest.

Unlike the other trees he was still very much on the short side. When a deer came wandering through the forest looking for a tasty snack, the fir tree's leaves were just within reach.

Snip! Snap! Soon every leaf was gone.

Oh, why didn't I just stay as I was! the little fir tree wondered.

Night came. The little fir tree slept. And when he woke next morning, he was back where he'd begun, dressed in his old coat of evergreen needles.

The difference this time was that he was happy.

A Winter's Tale

There was a man who lived by a churchyard. It didn't bother him one bit. 'Dead is dead,' he said. 'What harm can the dead do to me?'

But then, one cold midwinter's night, as he was on his way to bed, he heard a voice outside, calling his name.

He went to the window and looked out.

He couldn't see anyone out there.

'Who's there?' he cried. 'Who wants me?'

He heard his name called again from the graveyard.

So downstairs he went and out of the door.

Still the voice went on calling his name.

Across the graveyard he went towards it.

And tumbled straight into an open grave.

As he picked himself up he felt a bony hand on his shoulder and close to his ear he heard the same voice that had called his name. 'You won't get out,' it said. 'I've tried.'

You won't get out, it told him. But he did! He was so scared, he leapt straight up the side of that six-foot hole and out of it and didn't stop running till he was safe home again with the door locked and bolted.

They fished out his friend, half dead with cold, next morning from the open grave into which he'd tumbled while taking a short cut home from the Christmas Eve party in the pub the night before.

Brer Rabbit's Christmas

Carrot soup was Brer Rabbit's favourite meal. Carrot soup was what he was planning to have for his Christmas dinner until, just a few days before Christmas, he came home to find his whole crop of carrots gone! It wasn't hard to discover where they'd gone. The trail of dirt led straight to Brer Fox's house.

Brer Rabbit knocked on Brer Fox's door.

'Go away!' Brer Fox called from inside.

'Open this door!' yelled Brer Rabbit, kicking it. 'And give me back my carrots!'

'Your carrots?' said Brer Fox. 'I don't think so! The only carrots here are mine.'

'You don't even like carrots, you thief! You—you—you fox!'

'I don't, but some of my friends do. I'm inviting a few of my friends round for Christmas dinner, but not you, Brer Rabbit. You're bound to start a fight.'

'Is it a fight you want? Come out then and fight me!'

Brer Rabbit pummelled and kicked the door till his fists and toes were sore. Of course Brer Fox didn't open it. Brer Rabbit limped off home, vowing to have his revenge. And by the time he got there he was smiling. He had a plan!

Over the next few days he collected a bag full of rubbish. On Christmas Eve, he quietly set a ladder up against the wall of Brer Fox's house, climbed silently up onto the roof and stuffed the bag of rubbish down the chimney.

Before long Brer Fox's house was so filled with smoke he had to fling open the window in order to breathe.

'Hello, there, Brer Fox! It's Father Christmas!' cried Brer Rabbit, disguising his voice. 'I've got a sackful of presents here with your name on them, but they seem to have got stuck in the chimney. Can you reach up and give it a tug?'

'I'll have to put the fire out first!'

'Well, go on, then. I haven't got all night.'

So Brer Fox put out the fire and reached up the chimney for his bag of presents, while Brer Rabbit slid down the ladder and in through the window. He stole back his carrots and helped himself to the rest of the Christmas dinner Brer Fox had been preparing.

Off went Brer Rabbit, lickety-split, down the road, while Brer Fox was still tugging away at the sack that was stopping up the chimney, till at last the sack gave way and he tumbled back down into the fireplace along with the sackful of rubbish. Christmas morning came and with it Brer Fox's friends, but he'd no Christmas dinner to offer them.

From down the road, though, at Brer Rabbit's house, came a most enticing smell of carrot soup, plus roast turkey, Christmas pudding and mince pies.

'This way! Come in!' called Brer Rabbit. 'You're all just in time for dinner. Not you, though, Brer Fox. You're bound to start a fight.'

Food for Thought

Remember—a dog isn't just for Christmas.
The leftovers can make a very tasty snack on
Boxing Day!

Overheard on Christmas Eve

'I don't care who you are. If you don't get those reindeer off my roof before I count to ten, I'm going to call the police!'

A Visit from Santa

The house creaked. The roof leaked. The wind blew in and out through the broken window panes. There was no money for presents that year, or decorations, but we did what we could with holly and ivy and mistletoe plucked from the hedgerows. And when we found a poor old man who'd sat down for a rest on our doorstep on Christmas morning, 'Come in!' said Dad. 'And warm yourself by the fire.'

'Would you like some breakfast?' said Mum. 'It's only porridge, I'm afraid.'

'I love porridge!' he said and it was clear he did, because he polished it off so the bowl hardly needed washing.

Then he curled up on our sofa and slept the rest of the morning.

When he woke up, 'It's getting chilly in here,' he said.

It was. We couldn't afford proper logs for the fire, only the sticks we could gather by hand. Dad was on the point of sending me out for more when the old man said, 'Let me help.' He broke his walking stick into pieces and flung them onto the fire and soon the room was as warm as anything. I don't know what sort of wood that stick was made of but it was still burning brightly long after the old man had left.

'Well, I'm about ready for my Christmas dinner,' he said.

Mum got all embarrassed. 'You're welcome to stay for dinner,' she said. 'But it's just an old boiling fowl with a few vegetables thrown in.'

'Really?' he said. 'I could have sworn I could smell roast turkey. Have you looked in the oven lately?'

Mum looked in the oven and there was a roast turkey with all the trimmings. Stuffing and sausages, roast potatoes and parsnips too. I could see her puzzling away as she served it out, thinking of all the people we knew who might have slipped in with a full Christmas dinner while none of us was looking. Saw her coming to the conclusion: impossible! Still waste not, want not.

And when it came to the pudding, 'Have you left the stove on?' he said.

'I don't think so,' said Mum. But when she went to check, there was a proper Christmas pudding bubbling away in the pan.

It was our best Christmas dinner ever. That old man, he was the life and soul of the party. The last thing he said before he went was, 'By the way, when I'm short of cash, the first place I look is under the sofa cushions!'

Everyone else turned to look at the sofa. So I was the only one who saw what happened next. The others said afterwards he just walked out of the door, which slammed and set the dust swirling in the grate.

I know what I saw. I saw him fly straight up the chimney. I heard the jingle of sleigh bells and a voice calling out, 'Merry Christmas!' But I knew they'd never believe me, even after they found that bag of money he'd left stashed under the cushions on the sofa, enough to put the house right and pay off everything we owed. I know who our visitor was that Christmas. And so do you. Don't you?

Dumb Cake

Someone had put the idea in Bessie's head that if she made what's called a dumb cake on Christmas Eve, ate half of it, walked backwards upstairs to bed—all without saying a word (that's why it's called a dumb cake)—then put the other half under her pillow, she'd dream of the lad she was going to marry.

'So isn't she coming to the dance?' I said to Nell. 'Are you not coming, Bess?'

Bessie looked at me and shook her head. Playing dumb.

'You might have warned us, Bess! I told the lads to meet us here. Now there'll be three of them and only two of us. Maybe she could come anyway and just not speak?'

'Fat chance of that!' said Nell.

Bessie said nothing.

I took a lick of the mixture she'd left in the mixing bowl. It seemed to be mostly salt.

I said, 'Are you sure you got the recipe right, Bess? You're never going to eat this?'

Still Bessie said nothing. She lifted her precious dumb cake out of the oven, cut it in half, blew on it to cool it, then took a bite.

'Urrggh!' she said.

'You spoke!' I said.

'I did not!' cried Bessie.

'You did then,' said Nell. 'Never mind, Bess. I know a better way of finding out who you're going to marry. Come on upstairs and I'll show you.' So up we went to Bessie's bedroom. Nell sat her down facing the mirror, lit a candle and set it down in front of her and turned off the light.

'Look in the mirror,' whispered Nell. 'Don't look round or you'll break the spell. Look deep into the mirror, Bess, and you'll see the face of your true love looking over your shoulder.'

I don't think Nell actually planned what happened next.

It was me, not Nell, that left the outside door unlocked so the lads could come in without knocking if they arrived before we were done. It just happened to be Fred who arrived first and took it into his head to creep upstairs so he could surprise us.

He saw Bessie staring into the mirror and the two of us standing watching, quiet as mice. Naturally he crept forward to see what Bessie was looking at. Bessie caught sight of him staring at her over her shoulder in the mirror. 'Oh!' she said.

And with that 'Oh!' Fred's fate was sealed, though I dragged him back and the other lads arrived not a moment later, storming up the stairs, so when Bessie turned round it looked as if all three of them had arrived together. Still she'd no eyes after that for any of them but poor Fred.

They're coming up to their Diamond Wedding Anniversary next year. One thing that's always puzzled me though: if she had eaten that dumb cake and slept with it under her pillow that night, would she have dreamed of Fred? Or someone else? Or nobody at all. That's something I'll never know.

White Christmas

A re we going to have a white Christmas? Isn't that what we'd all like to know? Isn't a white Christmas what we all hope for every year? Sadly, with all their satellites and computers, the best the weathermen can predict is no more than a few days ahead.

Native peoples, so they say, can do much better, though how they do it is a mystery. In the old days, knowing what the weather was going to do well in advance could make the difference between life and death for the whole tribe. But the new chief on the reservation was college educated. He didn't know the old ways. So when the tribal elders came to him asking what provision the tribe should make for the coming winter, he did the modern thing. He phoned up the local weather station.

'Is it going to be a cold winter?' he asked.

'Oh, yes,' said the weatherman. Saying the winter was going to be cold was a pretty safe bet, since winter is generally colder than summer.

So the young chief went back to the tribe and told them to start stocking up for a cold winter. Then, since he felt he ought to add something to that (since winter can usually be relied on to be pretty cold), he told to them to stock up on extra firewood.

Winter came and it was unusually mild. The young chief phoned the weatherman again. 'I thought you said it was going to be a cold winter,' he said.

'So I did,' said the weatherman.

'But it's not.'

'It will be. Just wait and see.'

The young chief went back to his tribe and told them to stockpile every stick of wood they could find.

December came and still the weather continued unseasonably mild.

Again the young chief called the weatherman. 'You told me it was going to be a cold winter,' he said.

'It will be. The cold snap's coming very soon.'

'How soon?' The young chief tried to help him out. 'Would you say by Christmas?'

'Oh!' said the weather forecaster. 'Are we going to have a white Christmas? Is that what you want to know? Well, I'd say the signs are pretty good. I drive past the reservation every day on my way to work. Those Native Americans know a thing or two about predicting the weather. And they're stock piling wood this winter like I've never seen them do before!'

Christmas 1683

Winters were colder in those days. In centuries to come, men would call it the Little Ice Age. Of course, we didn't know that at the time. That year it was so cold, the smoke from the chimney fires never rose above the rooftops. The only place you could breathe easy was down by the river, so that's where I went most days. I saw how the ice was building up. At first there were just little chunks of it, bobbing about on the water. Then the chunks got bigger and there were more of them, until some of the boats trying to cross got stuck and had to be pulled off by ropes thrown from the shore and the watermen said they'd go no more.

The only way to cross the river then was Old London Bridge. Nineteen piers it had, which didn't leave much space for the water to flow through even in summer.

Now, as the ice built up round the piers, the water was down to a trickle. Then it was down to nothing—though you could still hear it flowing under the ice, if you stopped to listen.

After that there was no stopping the ice from building up further and further back along that mighty River Thames.

Soon there were men walking across it dry-shod and very proud of themselves, but still picking their feet up daintily like well-schooled horses lest the ice give way under them.

Pretty soon after that the first booth was set up on the ice, offering mulled wine and gingerbread to the brave spirits who'd made the crossing.

Maybe it was because it was Christmas and everyone was in a holiday mood. Maybe it was because the air was so foul in the city. Within days there were streets of booths set up on the ice, selling brandy balls and gingerbread, hot pies, puddings and pancakes and souvenirs. Soon there were puppet plays and fire eaters and sword swallowers and men on stilts. Some say there was a fox hunt, though I never saw it. There was even an ox roasted whole on the ice!

And I saw the king! King Charles himself came to see the Frost Fair on the Thames with all his lords and ladies. And had his name set down on a certificate by Master Croom, who'd set up his press there on the ice, as proof that he'd been there. As if anyone would argue with the king, if he said that he had!

I know it was a terrible winter for some, with many folks starving and freezing to death in their own homes and farmers ruined, their sheep and cattle frozen dead in the fields, and post boys, too, found stone cold dead in the saddle when the thaw came, and their horses under them.

All I truly remember is the wonder of it—the excitement! Of that great City of London celebrating Christmas on the River Thames!

The Gift of Fire

It was early on Christmas morning, and cook was throwing a wobbly in the castle kitchen. The fire was out. Not a spark of life left in it. And on Christmas morning, too! No fire on Christmas morning meant bad luck for the coming year.

In vain she struggled to strike a light from her tinderbox (for this was in the days before anyone thought of inventing matches). 'Don't just all stand there!' she yelled. 'Find me a light from somewhere.' But all over the castle it was the same. The bedroom fires waited in vain for a taper from the kitchen fire to light them.

The king stood shivering in his underwear. 'Find me a light for the fire!' he commanded. 'I don't care what it costs!' There were plenty of people willing to offer a few coals for the royal fire as soon as word got round the town that cost was no object.

'A light for his majesty's fire?' said the Prime Minister. 'Help yourself—there's just one thing. There's this little estate in the country I've had my eye on…'

'Coals for His Majesty?' said the captain of the guard. 'My pleasure—now, about my promotion…'

'One gold piece for each lump of coal,' said the merchant.

'That's my price, take it or leave it.'

There was no shortage of coals. The trouble was keeping them lit. None of them made it back to the castle.

Then a page boy came to a little house at the far end of town. He knocked and went in and found a girl stirring porridge over a tiny fire. 'Come in and get warm,' she said. 'Would you like some porridge?'

The place was so snug and so warm—and the porridge so good!—the page boy almost forgot why he'd come, but when he told her about the problem with the castle fire, 'Take whatever you need,' she said.

'Don't you want anything for it?' he asked her.

'Of course not,' she said. 'Don't be silly.'

The page boy took one coal from the fire and even then he felt bad about taking it, the fire was so small (though deliciously warm!) but he put it in his lantern and hurried back to the castle.

To his surprise that single coal was burning more brightly than ever when he reached there. Soon the kitchen fire was blazing, the kettle was singing and—wonder of wonders!—the cook went about her work with a great big smile on her face. Everyone that day seemed to be smiling, wishing one another, 'Merry Christmas!'

It was only afterwards, when they came to wonder why one small piece of coal had kindled such warmth throughout the castle, they came to the conclusion that it must be because that one coal had been given without any thought of reward, in the true spirit of Christmas.

Waiting for Santa

'Go to sleep, George,' said his mother. 'Santa won't come if you're not asleep.'

'How will he know?' demanded George. 'How will he know I'm not asleep if he's not here to see me?'

'Just go to sleep,' sighed his father.

'How's he supposed to get into the house anyway?' said George. 'We haven't got a chimney.'

'He'll find a way,' said his father.

'Because he's magic!' beamed his mother. 'Now go to sleep.'

'Please go to sleep.'

George had no intention of going to sleep. He wanted to see Santa for himself. He wanted to see how Santa got into the house.

The next thing he knew, midnight was striking. He felt for the stocking at the end of his bed and found it stuffed full of presents. Santa had been and he'd missed him, the same as last year and the year before.

Then he heard the creak of a floorboard on the landing. Maybe it wasn't too late to see him.

George slipped out of bed and crept to the door.

He opened it and peeped out.

Looked left and looked right.

And saw no one.

Then he heard what sounded like footsteps in the attic above him.

He crept to the foot of the attic stairs and saw the attic door, which was always kept closed, standing ajar.

In his bare feet he crept upwards, step by step, till he came to the door, where he stopped and listened, holding his breath.

There was definitely someone—was it Santa? Please let it be Santa!—definitely someone moving about inside.

As he pushed the door open the cat ran out past him and down the stairs.

George stepped into the attic—and screamed.

AAAARRRRGGGHHH!

And so would you, if you stepped on a nail in your bare feet!

Christmas 1818

Mice!

In the little church of St Nicholas in the village of Oberndorf the pastor, Josef Mohr, finally gave up trying to get so much as a note out of the poor old church organ.

He'd nothing against mice. They were God's creatures too. They had their place in the world, but why, every winter, did they seem to think that that place was inside the St Nicholas church organ?

Now it was Christmas Eve and too late to get someone in to mend it till after the holidays. It wouldn't be much of a service tomorrow without the organ to help the singing along.

Unless his friend, the choirmaster Franz Gruber, could come up with some bright idea. He ought to give him fair warning, anyway, that the choir would be singing unaccompanied tomorrow. Break the bad news tonight.

So off he went, trudging through the snow, till he reached the top of the hill above the village. There he paused and turned round to look back.

It was a fine night. The sky above him was covered with stars. Below him the houses lay sleeping, smoke lazily curling from their chimneys, calling to mind for some reason he couldn't explain the first lines of a poem he'd written two years before. *Silent night. Holy night. All is calm…*

How did the rest of it go? He'd read it out in church that Christmas—he always liked to introduce something a bit different to each Christmas service—and he fancied it had gone down quite well. Still it had seemed to him that it lacked something—until now! Maybe, he thought. Then, why not?

His step was light as he made his way down the other side of the hill. By the time he reached Franz Gruber's house he was so out of breath, it was hard for the choirmaster to make sense of what he was trying to say: 'I thought if you could write some music to fit the words—'

'What words? By tomorrow? Do you know what time it is?'

'Something simple. Not for the organ. I thought—just a simple accompaniment on your guitar.'

'You want me to play the guitar in church?'

'A guitar has got to be better than nothing!'

'I might as well take a look at that poem of yours.'

And so it was, that on Christmas morning the astonished congregation in the little church of St Nicholas came to be the first people in the world to hear what is now the world's favourite Christmas carol. *Silent night, holy night…* All because of the mice who chose to make their nest that winter inside the St Nicholas church organ.

No More Christmas!

There was once a king who hated Christmas.

When he was little, he longed for a flying carpet that would carry him to magical lands. But all he got was a book of fairy tales.

He asked for the moon to play with. But all he got was a silver ball that wouldn't bounce. He dropped it on his foot and it hurt like billy-o.

So when he grew up he said, 'There will be no more Christmas!'

Soldiers marched through the town, the drummer boy at their head.

Ratatata! No presents! No toys!
No oranges for the girls and boys!

They tore down the mistletoe from the florist's shop and cleared the Christmas puddings and pies from the baker's window. They shut up the church and left the priest standing outside clutching his red umbrella.

Jehan the Fool sat moulding a piece of clay. 'What's that?' the drummer boy asked. 'Oh! It's me!' A tiny clay drummer boy, no bigger than his own thumb. He wished someone would give it to him for Christmas. But there wasn't going to be any Christmas. Not any more.

Off went the soldiers.

Rum-tiddle-tum!

No mistletoe ring!

No new-born king!

No new-born king? No baby Jesus? Jehan the Fool threw up his hands. 'What will happen then? Will it be winter for ever?'

'What rubbish you talk, Jehan the Fool! Run away and play with your bits of clay.'

It was, though, the coldest winter anyone could remember.

Christmas Eve was the coldest night yet. By his window the king sat, looking out over the frozen world.

Down in the street Jehan the Fool, called, 'Come!'

As if he was under some spell the king came, down the stairs and over the snow to the stable where he found the children gathered around the crib Jehan had made. There were the tiny figures of Mary and Joseph and the baby Jesus, no bigger than a thumbnail. There were the shepherds and the drummer boy... the priest with his red umbrella...the baker with his sack of flour for making the Christmas puddings and pies...the flower-seller with her sprigs of mistletoe... everyone was there. Not even the king had been forgotten.

As he knelt with the children beside the tiny crib, the ice in the king's heart melted into tears.

Back to the castle he skipped and ran, to order them to ring the bells. 'It's Christmas morning! Had you forgotten? Merry Christmas, everyone!' Where his feet trod a touch of green showed through the snow. And snowdrops, the first sign of spring.